If I had a fairy godmother, thought Brigid, *she'd appear right now.*

"Ohhh!" Brigid yanked back her hand.

A cat as big as an air conditioner stared at her through the open window.

Its enormous golden eyes held Brigid's eyes.

The silver bells on its collar flashed in the sun.

PRRRRR...

Brigid felt a tingling through her sneaker soles.

The cat's deep purring made the whole floor shake!

First Stepping Stone Books you will enjoy:

By David A. Adler
(The Houdini Club Magic Mystery series)
Onion Sundaes
Wacky Jacks

By Kathleen Leverich
Brigid Bewitched

By Mary Pope Osborne
(The Magic Tree House series)
Dinosaurs Before Dark (#1)
The Knight at Dawn (#2)
Mummies in the Morning (#3)
Pirates Past Noon (#4)

By Barbara Park
Junie B. Jones and the Stupid Smelly Bus
Junie B. Jones and a Little Monkey Business
Junie B. Jones and Her Big Fat Mouth
Junie B. Jones and Some Sneaky Peeky Spying

By Louis Sachar
Marvin Redpost: Kidnapped at Birth?
Marvin Redpost: Why Pick on Me?
Marvin Redpost: Is He a Girl?
Marvin Redpost: Alone in His Teacher's House

By Marjorie Weinman Sharmat
The Great Genghis Khan Look-Alike Contest
Genghis Khan: A Dog Star Is Born

By Camille Yarbrough
Tamika and the Wisdom Rings

Brigid Bewitched

by Kathleen Leverich

illustrated by Dan Andreasen

A FIRST STEPPING STONE BOOK

Random House New York

For Walter

—K. L.

Text copyright © 1994 by Kathleen Leverich
Illustrations copyright © 1994 by Dan Andreasen
All rights reserved under International and Pan-American Copyright Conventions.
Published in the United States by Random House, Inc., New York, and simultaneously
in Canada by Random House of Canada Limited, Toronto.

Library of Congress Cataloging-in-Publication Data
Leverich, Kathleen.
Brigid bewitched / by Kathleen Leverich ; illustrated by Dan Andreasen.
p. cm.
"A First stepping stone book."
Summary: When Brigid wishes for a fairy godmother to give her the courage to jump
off the high diving board, she encounters a large silver cat and a strange girl named
Maribel who gives her advice.
ISBN 0-679-85433-9 (pbk.) — ISBN 0-679-95433-3 (lib. bdg.)
[1. Fear—Fiction. 2. Jumping—Fiction. 3. Cats—Fiction. 4. Fairies—Fiction.]
I. Andreasen, Dan, ill. II. Title.
PZ7.L5744Br 1994
[E]—dc20 93-43221

Manufactured in the United States of America   10 9 8 7 6 5 4 3 2 1

Contents

1

Spellbound

That June morning Brigid Thrush had a problem.

She stared at herself in the bedroom mirror.

"...Mirror, mirror on the wall," said Brigid. "Send a fairy godmother to help me. Today. Now. Instantly!"

She waited for something to happen.

"*Your fairy godmother is busy!*" a voice boomed. "*Tell your problem to me.*"

Brigid stared. *Was* her mirror magic?

She turned to look behind her.

Her big brother stood at the bedroom door.

"*Gus!*"

"I thought you'd be at the park by now," said Gus. "At the pool. Jumping off the new high dive!"

Brigid sighed. The new high dive.

For weeks, no one had talked about anything else.

It was taller than the lifeguard's chair.

It was taller than the snack bar's roof.

It was fifteen feet tall.

Just thinking about it made Brigid feel sick.

High places scared Brigid.

Falling through space scared Brigid.

"You're not scared to jump, are you?" asked Gus.

"Me? Scared? I can't wait to jump," said Brigid.

Her knees shook as she sat on the floor.

Her hands shook as she pulled on a sneaker.

Gus gave her a hard look. "Because if you *were* scared, I'd give you some advice."

Brigid looked up. "What advice?"

"Jump anyway! Everyone will call you a baby if you don't!"

Gus laughed as he vanished into his own room.

"Very funny!" said Brigid.

She reached under the bed for her other sneaker.

She pulled it on and tied the laces.

Then she slumped back against her bed.

All her friends were dying to jump!

Jill. Lita. Wendy.

For days they had been talking about who would go first.

Brigid stuffed her red bathing suit into her backpack.

Why was she the only one who was scared?

Maybe I'm under an evil spell, thought

Brigid.

I need a fairy godmother to help me. She'd wave her magic wand—*Alakazam!* I'd jump off the high dive. No problem!

Brigid looked around for her swimming goggles. They weren't on the floor. Or on the night table. Then she saw them.

They were on the window sill where she'd left them.

Brigid reached for them.

If I had a fairy godmother, thought Brigid, she'd appear right now.

"Ohhh!" Brigid yanked back her hand.

A cat as big as an air conditioner stared at her through the open window.

Its enormous golden eyes held Brigid's eyes.

The silver bells on its collar flashed in the sun.

PRRRRR...

Brigid felt a tingling through her sneaker soles.

The cat's deep purring made the whole floor shake!

"Brigid!" Her father called from the front yard.

He sounded a million miles away.

"Your friends are here."

Brigid tried to move.

But she couldn't.

She tried to answer.

But she couldn't.

All she could do was stare at the cat.

Its fur was the color of silver smoke.

Its tail curled around its body like fog.

Its whiskers twitched. Sparks seemed to fly from their tips.

"Bri-gid?"

Brigid's heart pounded.

Her arms and legs felt like stone.

"Bri-gid!" Gus yanked open her door.

The cat turned.

It jumped from the roof.

There was a streak of silver and a *tinkle* of bells. Then it was gone.

Gus peered in at Brigid. "Didn't you hear

Dad? Hey, what's the matter? You look as though you'd seen a ghost."

Brigid's legs shook.

Her arms felt limp as cooked spaghetti.

"Gus, could I have a fairy godmother?"

"*Fairy godmother?*"

Gus put an arm around Brigid's shoulder.

He gave her a gentle shake.

"Ask yourself, Brigid. If you had a fairy godmother, would you be living in a house like this? Would you have a brother like me?"

"*Bri-gid!*" Her father was calling again.

Brigid sighed. "I guess not. I just thought I'd check."

"Enjoy the high dive!"

Brigid sighed again. "Right."

She snatched up her goggles and hurried downstairs.

2

Cats, Dogs, and Doubts

Brigid stepped outside.

Everything *looked* normal.

Her mother and father were doing yard work.

Her little sister, Patience, sat in a wading pool.

The family dog, Badboy, lay in the shade of a tree.

There was no sign of a cat.

Jill, Lita, and Wendy were waiting for Brigid.

"Off to the pool?" Mrs. Thrush called from the flower bed.

Mr. Thrush was trimming the hedge.

"Going to try out the new high dive?" he asked.

"We can't wait! It's fifteen feet high," said Wendy.

"It's going to be like jumping from a second-floor window!" said Jill.

"When can I go off the high dive?" said Patience.

Patience was five.

She was cute.

She was spoiled.

Patience splashed water from her wading pool at Badboy. "When?"

Mr. Thrush mopped his forehead. "Don't you think you should learn to swim first?"

"I know how to swim."

"That's news," said Brigid.

"I can swim a lot better than Baxter Cameron."

"Baxter's only six months old," said

Mrs. Thrush.

"I can swim better than Badboy."

Mr. Thrush laughed. "I doubt that. Badboy's a swimming champ."

Badboy lay peacefully in the grass. Patience scowled at him. "I can swim better than a *CAT!*"

Badboy sprang to his feet.

RRUFF-RRUFF-RRUFF! he barked.

"You've been told not to say that, Patience!" said Mrs. Thrush.

RRUFF-RRUFF-RRUFF!

"What's wrong with your dog?" Wendy asked Brigid.

"Cats drive him crazy!" shouted Brigid. "Even the *word* makes him upset."

RRUFF-RRUFF-RRUFF!

"And Patience likes to tease!" she added. "Let's go."

Brigid and her friends headed down Day Street.

They crossed Summer Avenue.

"Did you see that?" said Lita.

"What?" said Jill.

"Running up the hill. A cat. Silvery. And strange."

The hair on the back of Brigid's neck rose.

Jill said, "I didn't see any cat. Besides, nothing runs up this hill."

They trudged up Spy Hill.

At the top, they rested.

The park lay far below them.

Doll-size duck pond. Doll-size tennis courts. Tiny playground. Tiny swimming pool.

Down the hill they ran.

"At the pool let's play Follow-the-Leader," shouted Wendy.

They ran through the park gate and onto a path.

"I'll be leader!" yelled Jill.

Wendy stopped short. "It was my idea. I'll go off the high dive first."

"It'll be just like the Olympics!" said Lita.

"It'll be just like Acapulco!" said Jill.

"Acapulco?" said Brigid.

Wendy said, "People there dive into the ocean from a giant cliff!"

"Sometimes they hit the rocks and die!" said Jill.

Brigid swallowed hard.

She couldn't jump. What was she going to do?

Brigid wished as hard as she could. *Please, fairy godmother! Appear here! Appear now!*

"Hey!" Jill pointed down the path to the little kids' play area. "Who's she?"

3

Nobody's Cousin

A strange girl was sitting in the little kids' sandbox.

But she was no little kid.

She was their age.

"Where did she come from?" whispered Jill.

"Never seen her before," said Wendy.

"She doesn't go to our school," said Lita.

Jill said, "She doesn't live in our town. Maybe she's visiting."

"Darcy Benbow has a cousin," said Wendy. "Maybe that's who she is."

Brigid chewed her lip. "I don't know..."

The girl had light brown skin.

French-braided hair.

Spindly arms and legs.

She wore a silver T-shirt and silver shorts.

Silver bells jingled on her necklace.

Everything about her was just a little *strange*.

"I'd like to know what she's doing," said Lita.

They watched the girl pour water from a watering can.

She mixed the water into the sand.

She packed wet sand into a pail.

"She's making sand pies," said Wendy.

"Sand pies? Sand pies are for babies!" said Lita.

The girl turned the pail upside down.

She lifted it.

A perfectly shaped mound lay beneath.

The girl drizzled wet sand over the mound.

"Those aren't pies," said Jill. "She's building a sand castle."

"Not just a castle," said Lita. "She's putting in a courtyard, a pond, and people!"

Brigid blinked.

The landscape in the sandbox looked familiar.

A tiny pool. Tiny plastic people and trees.

Brigid swallowed hard.

"That's no castle. That's the pool house. And that's the pool. She's made a model of our park!"

"Brigid's right!" said Wendy. "Look at that Popsicle stick. She's even put in the new high dive!"

Lita sniffed. "Why would a girl who's not even from around here build a model of *our* park?"

"Magic?" said Jill.

"Alakazam!" giggled Wendy.

Brigid shuddered.

She looked at the sandbox again.

The strange girl was gazing at them.

She caught Brigid's eye.

Her lips curled into a slow smile.

The hair on the back of Brigid's neck rose.

A cat rubbed against the inside of her chest.

"Well, *why?*" said Lita.

Brigid shook herself. "I don't know."

"Who cares why?" said Wendy. "I want to swim. Let's go."

Brigid hurried along behind the others.

Was that girl my fairy godmother? she wondered. Is she here to help me?

"It'll be like jumping from a second-floor window!" said Jill.

"It'll be like jumping from the Acapulco cliffs!" said Lita.

Brigid gulped.

She *hoped* that girl was her fairy godmother.

She was going to need all the help she could get!

4

Frozen Brigid

Sunlight sparkled off the water.

The smell of chlorine filled the air.

Brigid shaded her eyes to peer at the high dive.

It looked taller than the flagpole.

Taller than the park's hundred-year-old tree.

Taller than anything I want to jump from! thought Brigid.

Wendy jumped first.

She hunched her shoulders and held her nose.

Jill watched. "Wendy looks like a scared rabbit!" she said.

Lita went next.

She stepped off as though she were stepping off a curb.

She sped by, arms waving. "Ohhhh!"

Jill shook her head. "Lita looks worse!"

She nudged Brigid. "Show them how to do it."

"I think I might be getting a cold," said Brigid. "Maybe I'd better not jump."

Jill looked surprised. Then suspicious.

"You're not scared to jump, are you?"

Brigid swallowed hard. "Scared? Me? I can't wait to jump. I'll do it right now."

"Yea, Brigid!" said Jill.

Brigid grasped the high-dive ladder with clammy hands.

Her stomach churned as she began to climb.

One, two, three... The metal rungs dug into the bottoms of her feet.

Five, six, seven... The metal handrails

felt cool and smooth against her palms.

Brigid kept climbing.

Thirteen, fourteen, fifteen… She reached the last rung.

She swung herself up onto the platform.

The sun shone.

The water sparkled.

The breeze blew.

Brigid felt great.

Everyone was watching her.

Phwwweeet! Far below, a whistle blew.

Brigid gazed down at the little figure in the lifeguard's chair.

"You, there! Brigid!" shouted Kim.

Kim was the lifeguard.

She was also Gus's girlfriend.

"I don't want to see any hotshot stuff. No cannon balls. No can-openers. No flips."

Brigid nodded. *I promise.*

She drew a giant X over her chest. *Cross my heart.*

Very carefully Brigid let go of the handrails.

Very carefully she stepped onto the board's sandpapery surface.

She walked to the end. Then she carefully curled her toes over the edge.

The water of the pool shimmered far below.

It looked cool.

It looked blue.

Brigid bent her knees.

That water looked a million miles away!

Brigid tried to straighten her knees.

She couldn't.

She tried to bend her knees further.

She couldn't do that.

She couldn't blink.

She couldn't speak.

Brigid stared down at the water.

Jump! she told herself.

She wanted to jump.

She had to jump.

She couldn't jump.

Try as she might, Brigid couldn't move.

5

~~~

Cat and Mouse

That night Brigid stared at her dinner without eating.

"I'm sure it wasn't *that* bad," said Mrs. Thrush.

Gus chewed a roll and nodded his head.

"Oh yes it was! Brigid's the first person in history to get stuck on a diving board," he said. "Kim nearly called the fire department. She thought they'd need a hook-and-ladder truck to get Brigid down."

"Fire departments do all sorts of things," said Mr. Thrush.

Patience squirmed in her chair.

She looked at Badboy. He was asleep on the dining room rug. "You mean like when the fire truck came to our house? Like when that fireman climbed our tree? To rescue the Stewarts' caaa—"

Badboy's ears shot up.

"Patience!" warned Mrs. Thrush. "Don't say that word!"

Patience slumped back in her chair.

She crossed her arms and sulked.

Mr. Thrush said, "Never mind, Brigid. Lots of people are afraid of high places."

"None of those people was at the pool today," said Brigid. "Except me."

Mrs. Thrush said, "Even Jill said she felt nervous."

"Maybe," said Brigid. "But Jill jumped."

Gus shrugged. "Some kids may tease you a little. But who cares?"

"I care!" said Brigid.

She frowned. "There's another thing. I wanted to jump. I meant to jump. But something happened. An invisible force stopped me."

Patience blinked. "Magic?"

Gus grinned. "Alakazam!"

Mr. Thrush coughed.

Mrs. Thrush covered a smile with her napkin.

"You can laugh," said Brigid. "But it did!"

"Did you really have to *crawl* back?" asked Patience.

"On all fours," said Gus.

Brigid buried her face in her hands. "*Everyone* saw me. *Creeping* along like a— like a—"

"Cat!" cried Patience.

RRUFF-RRUFF-RRUFF! barked Badboy.

"That's enough, Badboy!" said Mr. Thrush.

RRUFF-RRUFF-RRUFF!

"Patience, you've been told not to say that word!" said Mrs. Thrush.

RRUFF-RRUFF-RRUFF!

"But—"

"Patience!" Mr. Thrush sounded angry.

"But there *is* one! See?"

Everyone looked where Patience pointed.

RRUFF-RRUFF-RRUFF!

Outside on the porch sat a cat as big as an air conditioner.

The cat didn't move when Badboy barked.

It didn't arch its silvery back.

It didn't blink its golden eyes.

"I've never seen such a large cat!" said Mr. Thrush.

The cat shook itself.

Its bell collar jingled. *Tinkle-tinkle...*

Mrs. Thrush frowned. "What's that in its mouth?"

"A mouse?" Patience sounded hopeful.
The cat laid something on the porch.
Then it gave Brigid a long look.
Tinkle-tinkle-tinkle... It ran off across the lawn.

Patience slid from her chair.

She ran to the porch door.

"Patience, come back to this table!" said Mr. Thrush.

Patience tugged open the door and stepped outside.

"Patience, do *not* touch that mouse!" warned Mrs. Thrush.

"It isn't a mouse!" Patience ran back inside.

She held up a small gray plastic figure. "It's a girl!"

Brigid looked.

It was a girl. A plastic girl. Wearing a plastic bathing suit and swimming goggles.

"It's mouse-colored, Brigid," said Patience. "But it looks just like you!"

Brigid had a funny feeling. The feeling that someone was sending her a message.

6

A Person with Powers

After dinner, Brigid said, "I have to go out for a minute."

She ran out the door and into the twilight.

She ran up Spy Hill and down the other side.

She ran through the park, into the playground, to the sandbox.

There sat the girl.

Brigid caught her breath. She held out the plastic figure. "Your cat left this at my house."

The girl gazed at Brigid out of odd,

golden eyes.

She raised an eyebrow. "Cat? What sort of cat? A large silver animal with a bell collar and golden eyes?"

Brigid felt a little dizzy. "That's the one."

The girl went back to molding sand. "Never seen it. I don't own a cat."

Brigid blinked. "If it's not yours, how did you know?"

"I know lots of things. I know that your name is Brigid Thrush."

Brigid stared.

"I know that you make wishes in mirrors."

Brigid gasped.

"I know that you have a problem. A fifteen-foot problem."

"The high dive," sighed Brigid.

"Exactly!" said the girl. "You can't jump."

"I wanted to jump!" said Brigid. "I

planned to jump. I would have jumped. An invisible force stopped me."

She waited to see if the girl would laugh.

The girl didn't laugh.

She nodded. "I know all about it."

Brigid blinked. "Am I under a magic spell?"

The girl turned a pailful of wet sand upside down.

She tapped firmly on the pail's bottom. "I dislike speaking of spells. I prefer to say you have a block. A mental block."

Brigid swallowed.

A spell must be a secret thing.

Something you weren't supposed to talk about.

She watched the girl remove the pail.

Underneath lay a perfectly molded wet-sand mound.

"How's a *block* stopping me from jumping off the board?"

The girl picked up a stick.

She started to draw with it in the sand.

"Look," she said.

She drew the profile of a person's head.

In the middle, where the person's brain would be, stood the wet-sand mound.

The girl sat back on her heels. She used the stick as a pointer. "That person is you," she said.

She pointed to the mound. "That's your mental block. We've got to smash it!"

She slammed down the stick.

Brigid grabbed her head.

The wet-sand mound collapsed.

The girl threw down the stick.

"I'll tell you how to jump," she said. "All you have to do is trust me."

Brigid let go of her head.

She felt shaken.

She felt nervous. "Trust you? I don't even know you."

The girl poured sand from one hand to the other.

She said, "Oh yes, Brigid. I think you do."

Once again, the hair on Brigid's neck rose.

Once again, a cat rubbed against the inside of her chest.

Brigid shivered.

"You know my name," she said. "What's
yours?"

The girl studied her sandbox landscape.

She was deciding where to put the plastic
figure of the girl.

"Maribel is my name," she said.

"Maribel?"

Carefully, Maribel balanced the figure on
the end of the tiny high dive.

The ground under Brigid's feet felt shaky.

As though she were standing in midair.

As though nothing held her but a narrow board.

"Maribel Jump."

Brigid stared at the girl. "Your last name is *Jump?* You're kidding, right? What's your real name?"

Maribel turned her odd, golden gaze on Brigid. "*J—U—M—P. Jump.*"

She flicked the figure with her finger.

Splash! It landed in the tiny pool.

Brigid's clothes were drenched in sweat.

But the ground under her feet felt firm.

"Well, Brigid Thrush. Will you trust me?"

Brigid turned and ran as fast as she could.

She didn't stop until she reached home.

7

Breaking the Spell

The next morning Brigid was at the pool early.

She was there before it opened.

Gus and Kim were going to help her jump.

The two of them frowned at the high dive.

"Brigid's trouble is, she's doing too much, too fast," said Gus.

"She's got to work up to the high board slowly," said Kim.

She turned to Brigid. "We've only got ten minutes until I open the pool. Here's the plan. Start by jumping off the side of the pool."

Brigid walked to the pool's edge and jumped.

"Now jump from the regular board," said Gus.

Brigid climbed onto it.

She ran, bounced once, and jumped.

"*Now*, jump from the high board."

"I can't. I'll freeze."

"Brigid, this is *sure* to work."

Brigid sighed and started up the ladder.

When she reached the last rung, she swung herself onto the platform.

"Don't be scared. It's just like the low board. Only higher," yelled Gus.

"A lot higher," muttered Brigid.

"Let's go, Brigid! You can do it!" called Kim.

Brigid shook out her arms and legs.

She pulled down the back of her red bathing suit.

She gave herself a pep talk.

It's just like the low board, only higher. It's just like the low board, only higher. It's just like the low board...

She took a deep breath and walked out onto the high dive. She didn't stop until she reached the end.

"Looking good, Brigid!" yelled Gus.

"Go for it!" called Kim.

Brigid peered over the edge of the board.

The water of the pool shimmered far below.

It looked cool.

It looked blue.

Brigid bent her knees.

That water looked a million miles away!

"Jump, Bridge!" yelled Gus and Kim.

Brigid tried to straighten her knees.

She couldn't.
She tried to bend her knees further.
She couldn't do that.
Brigid stared down at the water.
Jump! she told herself.

She wanted to jump.

She had to jump.

She couldn't jump.

"I can't wait any longer, Brigid," cried Kim. "I have to let people in."

"Inch back, Brigid," cried Gus.

"Little step. Little step. That's the way."

Brigid inched.

She thought about the girl at the sandbox in the playground.

Maribel. Maribel Jump.

I can tell you how to jump.

All you have to do is trust me.

Brigid made up her mind.

She grasped the railing.

She scrambled down the ladder.

If she hurried, she could be at the sandbox in ten minutes.

Maribel was working on her sandbox landscape.

"Welcome back," she said to Brigid. "Are you ready to trust me now?"

Tinkle-tinkle. Her bell necklace jingled.

Brigid swallowed hard.

She nodded.

"All right! There are four things you have to do. First. Sleep upside down tonight."

"Upside down?" said Brigid.

"With your head at the foot of the bed and your feet at the head."

"Can I move my pillow down?"

Maribel considered for a minute. "When it comes to mental blocks, the smallest detail counts. Better not chance it."

Brigid chewed her lip.

She wondered if she would sleep *at all* without a pillow.

"Second. Don't wear your red bathing suit. Wear your blue one."

Brigid blinked. "I never wear that suit.

How did you know I had a blue one?"

"Third. When you reach the end of the high dive, stop. Spell your name backward."

Brigid frowned. "Thrush. H—R—No, wait. H—S—"

Maribel rolled her eyes. "Not your *whole* name. You'd be up there all day. Just the *Brigid* part."

"Brigid. D—I—*unh*—G—I—"

"Fourth. Stop here on your way to the pool tomorrow. I'll tell you the fourth thing then."

Brigid stopped spelling. "You promise you'll be here? You won't forget?"

"I never forget," said Maribel. "Ever."

Brigid turned to go.

"Wait," said Maribel. "Whatever you do, don't tell *anyone* about me. This plan won't work if you do."

"I won't!" promised Brigid. "Not a word. Cross my heart."

8

A Case of Amnesia

At dinner that night, Brigid was too excited to eat.

She was too excited to think.

Tomorrow she was going to jump off the high dive!

It was all she could talk about.

"I have to sleep upside down. I have to wear my blue bathing suit. I have to spell my name backward. There's a fourth thing. I don't know yet what it is."

"If I do all those things, can I jump off the high dive?" said Patience.

"Not until you learn to swim," said Mr. Thrush.

"My friend says this is sure to work," said Brigid.

"Just who is this friend?" said Mrs. Thrush.

Brigid opened her mouth to speak.

Whatever you do, don't tell anyone about me! This plan won't work if you do.

Brigid blinked.

She had forgotten Maribel's warning!

She had told her family everything.

Or nearly everything.

What would Maribel do if she knew?

Mrs. Thrush said, "Tell us about this friend. What's her name?"

Brigid ran a finger around the rim of her milk glass.

She screwed up her forehead as though she were thinking hard. "It's a *funny* name. A name I've never heard before."

She looked at her mother and shrugged. "I forget."

"Where does she live?" said Mr. Thrush.

"Who are her parents?" said Mrs. Thrush. "We like to meet the people you spend time with."

"Wel-ll—" Brigid twisted her napkin.

Mr. Thrush said, "Here's what we'll do. After dinner, Brigid can phone her friend. We'll speak to the parents."

Brigid froze.

Maribel wouldn't have a phone.

Maribel wouldn't have parents.

No fairy godmother would.

"What do you say, Brigid?"

Rrrrrrrrrr... Under the table, Badboy began to growl.

"What's wrong, boy?" said Gus.

Badboy sprang to his feet.

RRUFF-RRUFF! he barked.

"Patience!" Mr. Thrush glared.

Patience said, "I didn't say it!"

"Badboy, quiet!"

RRUFF-RRUFF-RRUFF!

"Look! Out on the porch."

"It's the same cat as last night!" said Mrs. Thrush.

The huge silver cat prowled back and forth outside the porch door.

Mr. Thrush said, "Why's it visiting us? Patience, did you feed it?"

"You always blame me!"

RRUFF-RRUFF-RRUFF!

"Brigid?"

The cat turned its golden gaze on Brigid.

Brigid couldn't help but gaze back.

She felt a little dizzy. "I don't think it's here for food. It's come for something else."

"Something else? What else?"

"There it goes!" said Mrs. Thrush.

As suddenly as it had appeared, the cat ran off.

Mr. Thrush shook his head. "Crazy animal. Now then, what were we talking about?"

Gus frowned. "It was something important."

Mrs. Thrush frowned. "Isn't that odd? My mind's a blank."

Patience stood on her chair. "I know! I—" She stopped.

She clutched her head and looked around, wide-eyed. "Someone's erased my brain!"

"Calm down, Patience," said Mrs. Thrush.

"We've all come down with amnesia!" Mr. Thrush acted as if he was joking. But there was something uncertain about his grin.

"Brigid, do you remember?"

The whole family turned to look at her.

Brigid blinked.

Remember? How could she forget? They'd been talking about Maribel. They'd been talking about Brigid's *phoning* her after dinner!

She put on a puzzled expression.

She shook her head.

She grinned. "Maybe that's why that cat came! To make us forget."

To her relief, everyone laughed.

9

The Fourth Thing

The next morning Brigid was in a terrible mood.

Her neck felt stiff as she trudged to the pool.

Her eyes felt red and scratchy.

The worst part of sleeping upside down was, *you didn't sleep!*

On Spy Hill she kicked every pebble in her path.

In the park she did not *Keep Off the Grass*.

The early morning dew made her sneakers soggy.

She had a bad taste in her mouth.

Most of all, she felt nervous.

How could sleeping upside down break a spell?

How could spelling backward help her jump off the high dive?

Just picturing the high dive made Brigid's stomach knotty.

She thought, What if I still can't jump? What if I get turned to stone like before?

She pulled open the playground gate.

She tried to make herself calm.

Soon everything will be fine, she told herself.

I'll see Maribel in a few minutes.

I'll learn the fourth thing in a few minutes.

A few minutes after that, I'll jump off the high dive!

She peered past the swings, seesaws, and jungle gym to the sandbox.

No one was there.

Brigid ran to the sandbox.

She looked all around.

No Maribel.

She peered down every path.

She even checked the branches of trees.

Maribel was nowhere to be seen.

She knows I talked about her! She's not going to tell me the fourth thing! thought Brigid.

If I don't know that, how am I going to jump?

Then she noticed.

In the sand.

A neatly printed message.

> 4. *After you spell your name*
> *backward, jump UP.*

Next to the message was a drawing of a

finger pointing skyward.

UP? thought Brigid.

That's the magic? That's Maribel's fourth thing?

Jump UP?

She sank to a seat on the sandbox's edge.

What I'd better do is *GIVE* up!

PRRRR...

Out of nowhere the silver cat appeared.

Its golden eyes blazed at Brigid.

Its purring sounded as loud as a motor-cycle.

Its silver tail waved angrily back and forth.

It arched its back and hissed.

Sparks flew from the tips of its whiskers.

"Uhhh!" Brigid drew back.

The cat hissed again.

Brigid understood what the cat was telling her.

Jumping UP might not solve her problem.

But *giving up* would certainly make it worse!

Brigid edged away from the cat.

She ran for the pool.

The sun shone.

The water sparkled.

The breeze blew.

Brigid let go of the handrails.

She pulled down the back of her blue suit.

She stepped up onto the board's sandpapery surface.

She walked to the end and curled her toes over the edge.

The water of the pool shimmered far below.

It looked cool.

It looked blue.

Brigid bent her knees.

That water looked a million miles away.

"Go, Brigid!"

"You can do it, Bridge!"

Brigid tried to straighten her knees.

She couldn't.

She tried to bend her knees further.

She couldn't do that.

Then she remembered the third thing.

"d—i—g—i—r—B," she spelled.

The day darkened.

The air turned cold.

The wind blew.

Brigid glanced upward.

A giant cloud had gathered in front of the sun.

Brigid's heart began to pound.

Part of the silvery cloud looked like a head.

A head with two small, pointy ears.

Beneath the head stretched a powerful four-footed body.

From the body's end curled a long silver tail.

Uh-oh, thought Brigid.

Two shafts of sunlight cut golden openings in the cloud.

The openings looked exactly like two golden eyes.

Brigid felt them glaring at her.

Sleep upside down.

Wear your blue suit.

Spell your name backward.

Without knowing how she did it, Brigid straightened her knees.

She threw up her arms.

In what felt like slow motion, she rose to her toes.

Jump UP!

"Ohhhhh—!" Brigid jumped.

10

The Sign

That night at dinner Brigid said, "I jumped all day! One jump after another. I didn't freeze. I wasn't afraid. No invisible power stopped me. I jumped *up* instead of *down*."

"Up. Down. What's the difference? Either way you land in the pool," said Gus.

Brigid shrugged. "When I thought *down*, I couldn't move. When I thought *up*, it felt easy."

"Maybe it's a magic spell," said Patience.

Brigid gave her a sharp look.

Gus said, "That friend of yours is pretty smart. What is she, Brigid? Some kind of a wizard?"

Wizard? Brigid shifted uneasily in her chair.

Everyone was looking at her.

Everyone was waiting to hear what she'd say.

She swallowed hard. "More like a fairy godmother, I'd say."

For a minute, everyone looked uncertain.

Then they laughed.

Mr. Thrush pushed back his chair. "Who's ready for dessert?"

Rrrrrrrrrr... growled Badboy.

"Patience!"

"I didn't say it!"

Badboy sprang to his feet.

RRUFF-RRUFF-RRUFF! he barked.

Everyone glanced out at the porch.

It was empty.

No cat prowled by the door.

Rrrrrrrrr…

"See, Badboy?" said Mr. Thrush. "False alarm."

RRUFF-RRUFF-RRUFF!

The hair on the back of Brigid's neck rose.

She had a feeling.

"Maybe I should take Badboy outside," she said. "Just to show him there's nothing there."

The rest of the family started to clear the table.

Brigid opened the door and stepped out.

Patience ran after her. "I'll go, too. Ohhhh—"

Patience stared up.

High in the branches of a tree sat Maribel.

She peered down at them.

Patience nudged Brigid. "Is that your friend? Is she the one?"

RRUFF-RRUFF-RRUFF!

Badboy stood under the beech tree and barked.

"That's enough, Badboy!" said Brigid.

RRUFF-RRUFF-RRUFF!

Patience ran to stand below Maribel's perch. "Badboy thinks you're a cat. He's supposed to be a watchdog. But he's not too smart."

RRUFF-RRUFF-RRUFF!

Maribel slid out of the tree.

She looked Badboy in the eye.

RRUFF-Rruuu—

Badboy stopped barking.

He rolled over on his back.

He stared up lovingly at Maribel.

Patience's eyes widened.

Maribel turned to Patience. "Not smart? Badboy's as smart as paint."

"Paint?" said Patience.

Maribel took Patience by the shoulders.

She looked Patience in the eye. "Go help your parents fix dessert."

"*Help?*" Patience gazed up at Maribel.

She blinked.

Without another word, she went into the house.

When they were alone, Brigid turned to Maribel. "You were supposed to meet me at the sandbox!"

Maribel cocked her head. "*You* were supposed to keep quiet about me!"

Brigid blushed. "I didn't mean to tell my family. I forgot."

Maribel clapped Brigid on the shoulder. "Here's the important thing. You jumped off the high dive. You smashed your mental block!"

"I did?" said Brigid.

A stick slammed down inside her head.

A sand mound collapsed.

"*Bri*-gid!" Her mother called from the house.

"Brigid, dessert's ready!" called her father.

Maribel turned to go.

"Goodbye, Brigid Thrush."

Brigid grabbed her arm.

"Wait!" she cried. "Where do you live? How can I find you? Are you my…"

Brigid let her voice trail off.

She'd feel foolish saying the words.

"Your fairy godmother?" said Maribel.

She looked Brigid in the eye. "What do *you* think?"

Brigid felt dizzier and dizzier.

She tightened her grip on Maribel's arm.

"*Bri*-gid!" Her mother called again.

Brigid turned to answer. "Coming!"

She turned back.

Her hand held thin air.

Tinkle-tinkle.

A silver cat ran up the beech tree, over the fence, and away.

Mr. Thrush stepped onto the porch.

"Didn't you hear us call you?"

Mrs. Thrush followed. "What a glorious evening!"

A swallow swooped past.

The sky darkened.

The first stars twinkled into view.

Patience pushed past her parents.

"Where did she go? Where's Brigid's friend?" she asked.

"Your friend was here?" said Gus.

Mr. Thrush said, "Why didn't you ask her in?"

Brigid thought, If Maribel's my fairy godmother, she'll be back. If I'm in trouble, she'll have to come. I'm her job!

"I did ask her in," said Brigid. "She had to go."

Mrs. Thrush gave Brigid a hard look.

"Are you telling us *everything* you know about this friend?"

If Maribel has powers, thought Brigid, she'll give me a sign.

"I don't know anything about her. That's the truth."

"Look!" cried Patience.

A huge golden moon rose over the trees.

"Like a giant cat's eye," said Mrs. Thrush.

A scattering of stars twinkled beneath it.

"Like a cat's collar! With lots of silver bells," said Patience.

The hair on the back of Brigid's neck rose.

"A cat as big as a car!" said Gus.

"A cat as big as a house!" said Patience.

"*Hey-yy—*," said Gus.

Mrs. Thrush nodded. "I was thinking the same thing."

"You've said that word half a dozen times," said Mr. Thrush.

Everyone looked under the tree where Badboy lay.

"*Cat!* Cat-cat-*cat!*" said Patience.

Badboy rolled over on his back.

He stretched. He yawned. He sneezed.

"I call that weird!" said Gus.

Overhead, the moon turned from gold to silver. Everyone stared at it. "I call it time to go inside," said Mrs. Thrush.

Brigid felt a little dizzy. "I call it—"

Magic is what I call it! thought Brigid. She hurried into the house for dessert.

About the Author

"Every crisis I weathered in my early school years shared two features," says Kathleen Leverich. "First, each crisis was a matter of life or death. Second, my parents assured me I'd forget it in a week. Now, nearly two thousand weeks later, I know my parents were wrong. The jealous rivalry, the strange fears, the fashion dilemmas—I remember each one in living color. And that's why I write the books I do."

Kathleen Leverich is the author of *Best Enemies*, *Best Enemies Again*, and *Hilary and the Troublemakers*. She lives in Somerville, Massachusetts, with her husband.

Don't miss the next Brigid book.

Brigid gritted her teeth.

She stepped into the cafeteria.

All the kids looked up from their lunch.

They stared.

Brigid heard whispers.

"What's she wearing?"

She heard snickers.

"She looks like a fortune-teller."

She heard giggles.

"Hey, Brigid, check your calendar. This isn't Halloween!"

Brigid thought, *If you're there, Maribel, turn me into a pumpkin! Please!*

From *Brigid in Style*
by Kathleen Leverich